For Erin

The SILLY SATSUMA © 2012
by Allan Plenderleith

First published in this format in 2012
Reprinted in 2013
Ravette Publishing Limited
PO Box 876, Horsham, West Sussex RH12 9GH

ISBN: 978-1-84161-366-6

The Silly Satsuma

by Allan Plenderleith

RAVETTE PUBLISHING

On Christmas day across the land,
girls and boys just like you run downstairs
to see what Father Christmas has left
under the tree.

If they've been **GOOD,** there will be lots of presents wrapped up with love and kisses.

But if they've been **BAD,** what happens then?...

This little boy is called Eric.
Eric Greenbogle.
But Eric is not a good boy.

He's a bad boy.

When Eric ran downstairs on Christmas morning, there were NO Christmas presents under the tree! AAAargh!

All he could see was something very small and round - a bright orange satsuma.

BLOBBY
BLOBBY
BLOB
BLOB

screamed Eric.

"I don't want a silly satsuma!
What can a silly satsuma do?" grumbled Eric.

"Merry Christmas!" said a voice.

It was the satsuma –
for he was no ordinary satsuma.
He was a magic satsuma.

"Santa has sent me to help you Eric!"

THPTPT!

"I don't need a silly satsuma!
What can a silly satsuma do?
Can it make you run fast like trainers do?
Is it sticky and gross like pots of goo?
Does it have lots of games like computers do?
NO!
What can a satsuma do?"

The satsuma smiled, wiggled his fingers
and WACKA WACKA BOING!
WACKA WACKA BOING!
WACKA WACKA BOING BOING BOING!

When Eric opened his eyes he found they were in an old people's home, surrounded by snoring grannies.

"Hey! Where am I? It smells of cabbage."

"Now Santa told me you like to run up to old ladies and shout Boo! That's not very nice is it Eric? Would YOU like that if you were an old lady?"

CLICK!

Eric laughed. "You silly satsuma! I'm not an old lady - so there!" Suddenly the satsuma clicked his fingers.

When Eric looked down he realised –
he was an OLD LADY!

Suddenly the snoring old ladies woke up, but they weren't sweet old ladies — they were ZOMBIE OLD LADIES!!

He tried to run away but his old lady legs were too stiff.

"I think I'm going to wee myself!"

"Help me satsuma! Please!"
The satsuma smiled, wiggled his fingers
and WACKA WACKA BOING!
WACKA WACKA BOING!
WACKA WACKA BOING BOING BOING!

When Eric opened his eyes he found
they were in a dark castle,
cold and very spooky.

"Hey! Where am I? It smells of socks."

"Now Santa told me you like to squash insects. That's not very nice, is it Eric? Would YOU like that if you were a tiny insect?"

CLICK! "E!"

Eric laughed. "You silly satsuma! I'm not a tiny insect - so there!" Suddenly the satsuma clicked his fingers.

When Eric opened his eyes,
he wasn't boy-sized any more
- he was insect-sized!

Suddenly there was a sound.

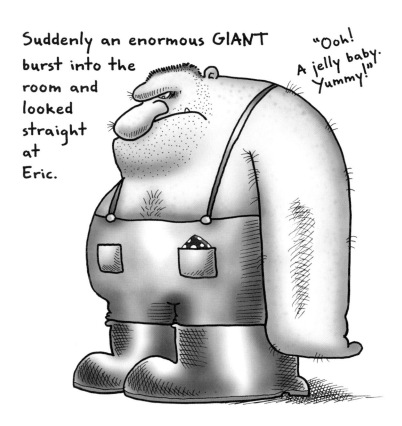

He lifted Eric up
and took him over to the table,
where there was a plate,
cutlery and a selection of dips.

He dipped
Eric's head
straight
into a big pot
of ketchup
and lifted him
up to
his mouth.

As Eric moved closer and closer to the giant's disgusting huge slobbery mouth, he screamed "Help me satsuma, please!"

The satsuma smiled,
wiggled his fingers
and...
WACKA WACKA
BOING!
WACKA WACKA
BOING!
WACKA WACKA
BOING BOING BOING!

When Eric opened his eyes
he found they were in a play park.
"Hey! Where am I now?
It smells of fresh air."
Eric shuddered.

"Now Santa told me you do something VERY naughty. Very naughty and very yucky."

"Santa told me you like to scoop up dog poop - and throw it at girls!

EURGH!

That's not very nice now is it Eric? Would YOU like that done to you?"

Eric was just
about to say
"You silly satsuma!
I'm not a girl - so
there," when he
stopped
and shouted:

"Hey! Wait a minute!
You're not going to
turn me into a girl
are you?! I couldn't
stand it!"

"No I'm not," said the satsuma.
"But how would you like to be
a poor little defenseless...

CLICK!

The satsuma clicked his fingers and
Eric turned into a small, smelly doggy plop.

Suddenly a huge spade lifted
Eric the poo. He tried to run away but
as you know, poos do not have any legs.

The spade threw him through the air and Eric the poo landed...

...right on top of a girl's head with a PLOP!

The satsuma smiled, wiggled his fingers
and WACKA WACKA BOING!
WACKA WACKA BOING!
WACKA WACKA BOING BOING BOING!

When Eric opened his eyes he was in his bedroom. "Stop! Please!! I'm sorry I've been a bad boy! I'm REALLY REALLY SORRY!!"

"You're not a bad boy Eric –
you're a good boy who made
bad choices."

Exhausted, Eric flopped onto his bed.
The satsuma tucked him in and gave
him a gentle pat on the cheek.
"Sweet dreams for a sweet boy."

And even though Christmas day
had only just begun, Eric
fell fast asleep.

The last thing he saw before he
closed his eyes was his friend the
satsuma smiling and waving goodbye.

Well, you may think
that is the end of our story.

But it isn't.

Not quite.

From that day on Eric was the
best boy you could ever wish to meet.

He was good to grannies.
He was terribly nice to tiny insects.
And he was lovely to little girls.

One year passed,
and Christmas morning had arrived.
Once again, Eric woke up early
and ran downstairs as fast as he could.

But this time Eric had been a good boy, and Father Christmas had brought him absolutely everything on his Christmas list!

The end.